Reprint Publishing

FOR PEOPLE WHO GO FOR ORIGINALS.

www.reprintpublishing.com

These verses of Mr. Bangs's have appeared from time to time in the various Harper Periodicals, and elsewhere.

OUT IN THE COLD

COBWEBS FROM A LIBRARY CORNER

By

John Kendrick Bangs

NEW YORK AND LONDON
HARPER & BROTHERS

MDCCCXCIX

TO

SISTER ANNE

CONTENTS

BOOKISH

	PAGE
A PESSIMISTIC VIEW	1
THE MASTER'S PEN—A CONFESSION	3
BOOKWORM BALLADS (A LITERARY FEAST)	5
IDEAS FOR SALE	8
THE AUTHOR'S BOOMERANG	11
TO AN EGOTISTICAL BIOGRAPHER	12
NO COPYRIGHT NEEDED	13
INGREDIENTS OF GREATNESS	14
A COMMON FAVORITE	15
THEIR PENS	17
AN UNSOLVED PROBLEM	18
THE BIBLIOPHILE'S THREAT	19
MY TREASURES	20
A POET'S FAD	21
THE POET UNDONE	22
A WANING MUSE	23
MODESTY	24
MY LORD THE BOOK	25
THE BIBLIOMISER	26
THE " COLLECTOR "	27

CONTENTS

	PAGE
A Reader	28
Fate!	29
A Pleasing Thought	30
Books *vs.* "Books," by a Bibliomaniac	31
A Confession	33
The Edition de Looks	35

WISE AND OTHERWISE

	PAGE
Napolini's Error	41
My Color	45
Contentment in Nature	47
The Heroic Gunner	49
The Pathetic Tale of the Caddy Boy	52
Garrulous Wisdom	56
The Perjury of a Rejected Lover	58
Maid of Culture	59
Not Perfect	60
A City Dweller's Wish	61
Where are They?	62
Memories	64
A Sad State	65
Ad Astra per Otium	66
Consolation	67
Satisfaction on Reading "Not One Dissatisfied," by Walt Whitman	68
To a Withered Rose	70
The Worst of Enemies	71

CONTENTS

	PAGE
JOKES OF THE NIGHT	72
AN AUTUMNAL ROMANCE	75
THE COUNTRY IN JULY	76
MAY 30, 1893	78
THE CURSE OF WEALTH	80
THE RHYME OF THE ANCIENT POPULIST	83
ONE OF THE NAMELESS GREAT	86
IN FEBRUARY DAYS	87
A CHANGE OF AMBITION	89
MESSAGE FROM MAHATMAS	91
THE GOLD-SEEKERS	95
ODE TO A POLITICIAN	98
SOME ARE AMATEURS	101

BOOKISH

A PESSIMISTIC VIEW

A LITTLE bit of Thackeray,
  A little bit of Scott,
A modicum of Dickens just
  To tangle up the plot,
A paraphrase of Marryat,
  Another from Dumas—
You ask me for a novel, sir,
  And I say, there you are.

The pen is greater than the sword,
  Of that there is no doubt.
The pen for me whene'er I wish
  An enemy to rout.
A pen, a pad, and say a pint
  Of ink with which to scrawl,
To put a foe to flight is all
  That's needed—truly all.

A   I

A PESSIMISTIC VIEW

But when it comes to making up
  A novel in these days
You do not need a pen at all
  To win the writer's bays.
A pair of sharpened scissors and
  A wealth of pure white page
Will do it if you have at hand
  A pot of mucilage.

So give to me the scissors keen,
  And give to me the glue,
And I will fix a novel up
  That's sure to startle you.
The good ideas have all been
    worked,
  But while we've gum and paste
There shall be books and books
    and books
  To please the public taste.

THE MASTER'S PEN—A CONFESSION

In my collection famed of curios
I have, as every bookman knows,
A pen that Thackeray once used.
　　To be amused,
I thought I'd "take that pen in
　　hand,"
And see what came of it—what
　　grand
Inspired lines 'twould write,
　　One Sunday night.
I dipped it in the ink,
And tried to think,
　　"Just what shall I indite?"
And do you know, that pen went
　　fairly mad;
A dreadful time with it I had.

3

THE MASTER'S PEN

It spluttered, spattered, scratched,
   and blotted so,
I had to give it up, you know.
It really wouldn't work for me,
And so I put it down ; but last
   night, after tea,
I took it up again,
And equally in vain.
      The hours sped ;
      I went to bed,
And in my dreams the pen came
   up to me and said :
"Here is the list of Asses who
   have tried
To take up pens the master laid
   aside ;
Look thou !" I looked, and lo ! —
   perhaps you've guessed—
My name, like Abou Ben's, led all
   the rest !

BOOKWORM BALLADS

A LITERARY FEAST

My Bookworm gave a dinner to a
    number of his set.
I was not there — I say it to my
    very great regret.
For they dined well, I fancy, if the
    menu that I saw
Was followed as implicitly as one
    obeys the law.

"'Twill open," he observed to me,
    "with quatrains on the half.
They go down easy ; then for soup"
    —it really made me laugh—
"The poems of old Johnny Gay"—
    his words were rather rough—
"They'll do quite well, for, after all,
    soup's thin and sloppy stuff.

"For fish, old Izaak Walton; and
to serve as an *entrée*,
I think some fixed-up morsel, say
from James, or from Daudet;
The roast will be Charles Kingsley
—there's a deal of beef in him.
For sherbet, T. B. Aldrich is just
suited to my whim.

"For game I'll have Boccaccio—
he's quite the proper one;
He certainly is gamey, and a trifle
underdone;
And for the salad, Addison, so fresh
and crisp is he,
With just a touch of Pope to give
a tang to him, you see.

"And then for cheese, Max Nordau,
for I think you'll find right there
Some things as strong and mushy
as the best of Camembert;
And for dessert let Thackeray and
O. Khayyám be brought,
The which completes a dinner of
most wondrous richness fraught.

BOOKWORM BALLADS

"For olives and for almonds we
   can take the jokes of *Punch*—
They're good enough for us, I
   think, to casually munch;
And through it all we'll quaff the
   wines that flow forever clear
From Avon's vineyards in the heart
   of Will of Warwickshire."

IDEAS FOR SALE

I'M in literary culture, and I've
    opened up a shop,
Where I'd like ye, gents and ladies,
    if you're passing by to stop.
Come and see my rich assortment
    of fine literary seed
That I'm selling to the writers of
    full many a modern screed.

I've bacilli for ten volumes for a
    dollar, in a bag—
Not a single germ among 'em that's
    been ever known to drag.
Not a single germ among 'em, if
    you see they're planted right,
But will grow into a novel that
    they'll say is out of sight.

I have motifs by the thousand,
    motifs sad and motifs gay.
You can buy 'em by the dozen, or
    I'll serve 'em every day :

8

I will serve 'em in the morning, as
the milkman serves his wares;
I will serve 'em by the postman,
or I'll leave 'em on your stairs.

When you get down to your table
with your head a vacuum,
You can say unto your helpmeet,
"Has that quart of ideas come
That we ordered served here daily
from that plot-man down the
street?"
And you'll find that I've been early
my engagement to complete.

Should you want a book of poems
that will bring you into fame,
Let me send a sample packet that
will guarantee the same,
Holding "Seeds of Thought from
Byron, Herrick, Chaucer, Ten-
nyson."
Plant 'em deep, and keep 'em wa-
tered, and you'll find the deed is
done.

IDEAS FOR SALE

I've a hundred comic packets that
    would make a Twain of Job ;
I have "Seeds of Tales Narcotic ;
    Tales of Surgeons and the Probe."
I've a most superb assortment, on
    the very cheapest terms,
Done up carefully in tin-foil, of my
    A 1 "Trilby Germs."

So perchance if you're ambitious
    in a literary line,
Be as dull as e'er you can be, you
    will surely cut a shine,
If you'll only take advantage of
    this opportunity,
When you're passing by to stop in
    for a little chat with me.

You may ask me, in conclusion,
    why I do not seek myself
All the laurel and the glory of
    these seeds I sell for pelf.
I will tell you, though the confi-
    dence I can't deny is rash,
I'm a trifle long on laurels, and a
    little short of cash.

THE AUTHOR'S BOOMERANG

HE frowns with reason ; he has always said,
"The public has no knowledge
of true art ;
The book of worth these days
would not be read ;
'Tis trash not truth that goes
upon the mart."

And then was published his be-
lovéd work—
Some twenty-six editions it has
had—
And he his own conclusion cannot shirk :
With such success as this it
must be bad !

TO AN EGOTISTICAL BIOG-
RAPHER

I'VE read your story of your friend's
    fine life,
  But really, gentle sir, I fail to see,
Why you have named it " Blank,
    and Jane his wife,"
  When you had better called it
    simply " Me."

NO COPYRIGHT NEEDED

I'VE penned a score of essays bright,
　In Addison's best style;
I've taken many a lofty flight,
　The Muses to beguile.

Of novels I have written few—
　I think no more than ten;
With history I've had to do,
　Like several other men.

And still, to my intense regret,
　Through all my woe and weal,
I've never penned a volume yet,
　A foreigner would steal.

13

INGREDIENTS OF GREAT-
NESS

THE style of man I'd like to be,
    If I could have my way,
Would be a sort of pot-pourri
    Of Poe and Thackeray;

Of Horace, Edison, and Lamb;
    Of Keats and Washington,
Gérôme and blest Omar Khayyám,
    And R. L. Stevenson;

Of Kipling and the Bard of Thrums,
    And Bonaparte the great—
If I were these, I'd snap my thumbs
    Derisively at Fate.

A COMMON FAVORITE

CHARLES LAMB is good, and so is
    Thackeray,
And so's Jane Austen in her pretty
    way ;
Charles Dickens, too, has pleased
    me quite a lot,
As also have both Stevenson and
    Scott.
I like Dumas and Balzac, and I
    think
Lord Byron quite a dab at spread-
    ing ink;
But on the whole, at home, across
    the sea,
The author I like best is Mr. Me.

A "first" of Elia filled my soul with
    joy,
A Meredith de luxe held no alloy.

And when I found *Pendennis* in
    the parts
A throb of gladness stirred my heart
    of hearts.
A richly pictured set of Avon's bard
Upon my liking bounded pretty
    hard;
But none brought out that cloying
    sense of glee
That came from that first book by
    Mr. Me.

And so I beg you join me in the
    toast
To him that I confess I love the most.
He does not always do his level best,
But no one lives who can survive
    that test.
His work is queer, and some folks
    call it bad,
And some aver 'tis but a passing
    fad;
But I don't care, the fact remains
    that he
Has won my admiration—dear old
    Me.

THEIR PENS

THE poet pens his odes and sonnets
  spruce
With quills plucked from the or-
  dinary goose,
While critics write their sharp in-
  cisive lines
With quills snatched from the fret-
  ful porcupines.

AN UNSOLVED PROBLEM

If Bacon wrote those grand inspir-
    ing lines
  At which alternately man weeps
    and laughs,
Who was it penned those chiro-
    graphic vines
  We know these times as Shakes-
    peare's autographs?

THE BIBLIOPHILE'S THREAT

IF some one does not speedily in-
    dite
  A volume that is worthy of my
    shelf,
I'll have to buy materials and
    write
  A novel and some poetry myself.

MY TREASURES

My library o'erflows with treasures
    rare :
    Of "Dickens' firsts," a full, un-
    broken set ;
And in a little nooklet off the
    stair
    The whole edition of my novel-
    ette.

A POET'S FAD

He writes bad verse on principle,
  E'en though it does not sell.
He thinks the plan original—
  So many folk write well.

THE POET UNDONE

HE was a poet born, but unkind
   Fate
  Once doomed him for his verses
   to be paid,
Whereon he left the poet-born's
   estate
  And wrote like one who'd hap-
   pened to be made.

A WANING MUSE

"Why art thou sad, Poeticus?"
   said I.
So blue was he I feared he would
   not speak.
"Alas! I've lost my grip," was his
   reply—
   "I've writ but forty poems, sir,
   this week."

MODESTY

"WHAT hundred books are best,
   think you?" I said,
   Addressing one devoted to the
   pen.
He thought a moment, then he
   raised his head:
   "I hardly know — I've written
   only ten."

24

MY LORD THE BOOK

A BOOK is an aristocrat:
  'Tis pampered—lives in state;
Stands on a shelf, with naught
    whereat
  To worry—lovely fate!

Enjoys the best of company;
  And often—ay, 'tis so—
Like much in aristocracy,
  Its title makes it go.

THE BIBLIOMISER

HE does not read at all, yet he
doth hoard
Rich books. In exile on his
shelves they're stored;
And many a volume, sweet and
good and true,
Fails in the work that it was
made to do.
Why, e'en the dust they've caught
since he began
Would quite suffice to make a de-
cent man!

THE "COLLECTOR"

I GOT a tome to-day, and I was
    glad to strike it,
Because no other man can ever
    get one like it.
'Tis poor, and badly print; its
    meaning's Greek;
But what of that? 'Tis mine, and
    it's unique.
  So Bah! to others,
  Men and brothers—
Bah! and likewise Pooh!
I've got the best of you.
Go sicken, die, and eke repine.
That book you wanted — Gad!
    that's mine!

A READER

DAUDET to him is e'er Dodett;
    Dumas he calls Dumass;
But prithee do not you forget
    He's not at all an ass;

Because the books that he doth
      buy,
    That on his shelf do stand,
Hold not one page his eagle eye
    Hath not completely scanned.

And while this man's orthoepy
    May not be what it should,
He knows what books contain, and
      he
    "Can quote 'em pretty good."

FATE!

I FEEL that I am quite as smart
As Edward Bulwer Lytton, Bart.

I'm also every bit as bright
As Walter Scott, the Scottish
knight;

And in my own peculiar way
I'm just as good as Thackeray.

But, woe is me that it should be,
They got here years ahead of me,

And all the tales I would unfold
By them already have been told.

29

A PLEASING THOUGHT

THEY speak most truly who do say
We have no writing-folk to-day
Like those whose names, in days
   gone by,
Upon the scroll of fame stood high.
And when I think of Smollett's
   tales,
Of waspish Pope's ill-natured rails,
Of Fielding dull, of Sterne too free,
Of Swift's uncurbed indecency,
Of Dr. Johnson's bludgeon-wit,
I must confess I'm glad of it!

BOOKS *vs.* "*BOOKS*"

BY A BIBLIOMANIAC

A VOLUME's just received on vellum
    print.
The book is worth the vellum—no
    more in't.
But, as I search my head for
    thoughts, I find
One fact embedded firmly in my
    mind.

That's this, in short: while it no
    doubt may be
Most pleasant for an author small
    to see
A fine edition of his work put out,
No man who's sane can ever really
    doubt

That products of his brain and pen
  can live
Alone for that which they may
  haply give !
And though on vellum stiff the
  work appears,
It cannot live throughout the after-
  years,

Unless it has within its leaves some
  hint
Of something further than the style
  of print
And paper—give me Omar on mere
  waste,
I'll choose it rather than some
  "bookish taste,"

Expended on a flimsy, whimsey tale,
Put out to catch a whimsey, flimsy
  sale.
I'd choose my Omar print on gro-
  cer's wraps
Before the vellum books of "bookish" chaps.

A CONFESSION

My epic verse, my pet production,
    which I deemed
  Sufficient to advance me to the
    highest peak
Of difficult Parnassus, goal of which
    I've dreamed
  For many a weary year, came
    back to me last week.
The Editor I cursed, that he should
    stand between
  My dear ambition and my scarce-
    ly dearer self ;
Whose unappreciation forced to
    blush unseen
  My one dear book, to gather dust
    upon my shelf.

33

That night in sleep an Angel fair
    came to my side,
    And in her hand she held a scroll;
    in lines of flame
The name of him I'd cursed was
    writ; and when I cried,
    "What portent this?" the rare
    celestial dame
                    Replied:
"Read here, O Ingrate base, the
    name of him thou'st cursed.
The very man of all men who
    should be the first
Thy love and lasting gratitude to
    know, since he
Still leaves the path Parnassian
    open unto thee—
A path which thou with halting
    rhyme, most ill composed,
Against thyself hast sought to keep
    forever closed.
Read thou thy lines again!"
             Ah! bitter was the cup.
I read, withdrew the curse — and
    tore the epic up.

THE EDITION DE LOOKS

How very close to truth these
    bookish men
Can be when in their catalogues
    they pen

The words descriptive of the wares
    they hold
To tempt the book-man with his
    purse of gold!

For instance, they have Dryden—
    splendid set—
Which some poor wight would part
    with wealth to get.

'Tis richly bound, its edges gilded
    —but—
Hard fate—as Dryden well deserves
    —*uncut !*

For who these days would think
  to buy the screed
Of dull old dusty Dryden just to
  read?

In faith if his editions had been kept
Amongst the rarities he'd ne'er
  have crept!

And then those pompous, overwhelming tomes
You find so oft in overwhelming
  homes,

No substance on a Whatman sur-
  face placed,
In polished leather and in tooling
  cased,

The gilded edges dazzling to the eye
And flaunting all their charms so
  wantonly.

These book-men, when they cata-
  logue their books,
Call them in truth *édition de luxe*.

THE EDITION DE LOOKS

That's all they have, most of 'em,
  just plain shape,
With less pure wine than any un-
  ripe grape.

But tomes that travel on their
  "looks" indeed
Are only good for those who do
  not read ;

And, like most people clad in gar-
  ments grand,
Seem rather heavy for the average
  hand.

WISE AND OTHERWISE

NAPOLINI'S ERROR

PIETRO NAPOLINI DI VENDETTA PAS-
QUARELLE
Deserted balmy Italy, the land
    that loved him well,
And sailed for soft America, of
    wealth the very fount,
To earn sufficient dollars there to
    make himself a count.
Alas for poor Pietro! he arrived in
    winter-time,
And marvelled at the poet who
    observed in tripping rhyme
How this New World was genial,
    and a sunny sort of clime.

No chance had he for music that's
    developed by a crank,
No chance had he at sculpture,
    nor a penny in the bank.

The pea-nut trade was languid,
and for him too full of risk;
He thought the work on railways
for his blood was rather brisk.
The sole profession left him to as-
suage his stomach's woe,
It struck him in meandering the
city to and fro,
Was surely that of shovelling away
the rich man's snow.

And then P. Napolini di Vendetta
Pasquarelle
Sought out a city thoroughfare,
the swellest of the swell.
He stole a shovel, and he found a
broom he thought would do,
Then rang the massive front-door
bell of Stuyvesant Depew.
"I wanta shov' da snow," he said,
when there at last appeared
Fitzjohn Augustus Higgins, who in
Birmingham was reared,
A man by all in low estate much
hated and much feared.

"Go wi," said Fitz, with gesture
   bold. "Yer cahn't do nothink ere,
Yer bloomin', hugly furriner!" he
   added, with a sneer.
"Hi thinks as 'ow you dagoes is
   the cuss o' this 'ere land,
With wuthy citizens like me 'most
   starved on every 'and.
Hi vows hif I'd me wi at all hi'd
   order hout a troop,
Hand send the bloomin' lot o' yer
   'ead over 'eels in soup.
Git hout, yer nahsty grabber yer;
   hewacuate the stoop."

Then when the snow had melted
   off, Fitzjohn Augustus went
And humbly asked his master for
   two dollars that he'd spent
In paying Napolini di Vendetta
   Pasquarelle;
While Nap went back to Italy, the
   land that loved him well,
Convinced that when he sailed
   that time his country to for-
     sake,

NAPOLINI'S ERROR

He must have got aboard the ship
  when he was half awake,
And got to London, not New York,
  by some most odd mistake.

44

MY COLOR

My best-loved color? Well, I think
    I like
  A soft and tender dewy green—
    for grass.
Sometimes a pink my fancy too will
    strike—
  In lobster *purée* or a Sauterne
    glass.

Blue is a color, too, I greatly love.
  It's sort of satisfying to my eyes.
'Tis their own color; and I'm quite
    fond of
  This hue also for soft Italian skies.

For blushes, give me red, nor hesi-
    tate
  To pile it on; I like it good and
    strong

MY COLOR

Upon the cheeks of her I call my
 Fate,
 The loveliest of all the lovely
  throng.

On golden - yellow oft my fancy
 dwells.
 'Tis almost godlike, as it sparkles
  through
The effervescent fizz ; and wondrous
 spells
 It casts o'er me when coined in
  dollars, too.

Hence, friend, it is I cannot specify
 What hues particular my joys
  enhance.
I like them all ; their popularity
 At special times depends on cir-
  cumstance.

CONTENTMENT IN NATURE

I would not change my joys for
    those
  Of Emperors and Kings.
What has my gentle friend the
    rose
Told them, if aught, do you sup-
    pose—
  The rose that tells me things?

What secrets have they had with
    trees?
  What romps with grassy spears?
What know they of the mysteries
Of butterflies and honey-bees,
  Who whisper in my ears?

What says the sunbeam unto
    them?
  What tales have brooklets told?

CONTENTMENT IN NATURE

Is there within their diadem
A single rival to the gem
  The dewy daisies hold?

What sympathy have they with
    birds
  Whose songs are songs of mine?
Do they e'er hear, as though in
    words
'Twas lisped, the message of the
    herds
  Of grazing, lowing kine?

Ah no! Give me no lofty throne,
  But just what Nature yields.
Let me but wander on, alone
If need be, so that all my own
  Are woods and dales and fields.

THE HEROIC GUNNER

When the order was given to withdraw from battle
for breakfast, one of the gun-captains, a privileged
character, begged Commodore Dewey to let them keep
on fighting until " we've wiped 'em out." — *War Anec-
dote in Daily Paper*.

At the battle of Manila,
  In the un-Pacific sea,
Stood a gunner with his mad up
  Just as far as it could be—
Stood a gunner brave and ready
  For the hated enemy.

Near the Isles of Philopena
  Raged the battle all the morn,
And the plucky Spanish sailors
  By the shot and shell were torn;
And the flag that floated o'er them
  To oblivion was borne.

THE HEROIC GUNNER

Every cannon belched projectiles,
  Every cannon breathed forth hell,
Every cannon mowed the foeman
  From the deck into the swell,
When amid the din of battle
  Rang the silvery breakfast-bell.

"Stop your shooting! Come to
    breakfast!"
  Cried the gallant Commodore.
"After eating we will let them
  Have a rousing old encore.
Stow your lanyards, O my Jackies;
  Let the cannon cease to roar."

Then upspake the fighting gunner:
  "Dewey, don't, I beg of you.
What's the use of drinking coffee
  Till we've put this scrimmage
    through?
If there's any one who's hungry,
  Won't this Spanish omelet do?

"Farragut would not have done it
  When through Mobile Bay he
    sped.

THE HEROIC GUNNER

Why then, Dewey, should we break-
    fast
  Till we've plunked 'em full of
    lead?
Let our motto be as his was—
  Damn the fishballs! Go ahead!"

THE PATHETIC TALE OF
THE CADDY BOY

"Come here," said I, "oh caddy boy,
  and tell me how it haps
You cling so fast unto these links ;
  not like the other chaps,
Who like to dally on the streets
  and play the game of craps?

"Is it that you enjoy the work of
  carrying a bag
While others speed the festive ball
  o'er valley, hill, and crag?
And do your spirits never seem to
  falter or to flag?

"I've watched you many a day, my
  lad, and puzzled o'er the fact
That you are so attentive to the
  game ; your every act

Doth indicate perfection — there's
been nothing you have lacked.

"And I would know just why it is
that you so perfect seem—
In all my golfing days you've been
the very brightest gleam—
Or am I lying home in bed and
are you just a dream?"

"Oh, sir," said he, "I caddy here
because I love my pa;
I cling unto these gladsome links
because I love my ma;
In short, I love my parents, sir, and
these my reasons are :

"'Twas but a year ago, good sir,
when first this ancient sport
Came in the portals of our home—
home of the sweetest sort ;
When golf came through the win-
dow, sir, why home went through
the port.

"My father first he took it up,
  and many a weary night
My mother with us children waited
  up by candle-light,
In hopes that he'd return and free
  us from our lonely plight.

"Then mother she went after him
  —alas! that it should be—
And shortly learned the game her-
  self—she plays it famously—
Which left us children orphans, I
  and all my brothers three.

"They play it here, they play it
  there, they play it everywhere;
No matter what the weather, be it
  wet or be it fair,
And for the cares of golf they've
  dropped their every other care.

"And so it is that we poor lads
  are forced to leave our home,
And join the ranks of caddy boys
  who o'er the fields do roam

PATHETIC TALE OF CADDY BOY

In search of little golf-balls in the
　　sunlight and the gloam ;

"For some day we are hoping that
　　our eyes again will see
Our most beloved parents on some
　　putting-green or tee ;
A sight to gladden all our hearts if
　　it should ever be."

And lo—I looked upon that boy—
　　his face was sweet and sad,
And to my heart there came a
　　twinge, for in that little lad
I recognized my eldest son—*I* was
　　that wicked dad !

And now together we are out on
　　links at home and far.
He and his three small brothers
　　with their shamed, repentant pa,
A-looking here and looking there
　　to find their dear mamma.

GARRULOUS WISDOM

I KNOW a wondrous man — my
   neighbor he;
   He's ripe in years, and great in
   understanding.
He's versed in art, and in philos-
   ophy
   He shows a mind that's verily
   commanding.

He'll stand before a painting, and
   without
   A single instant's thought, or
   hesitation,
He'll tell the painter's name, nor
   any doubt
   Is there he gives the proper in-
   formation.

The rocks, the hills and valleys,
    hold from him
  No secret that is past a man's
    revealing.
He knows why some are stout and
    others slim ;
  He comprehends all kinds of hu-
    man feeling.

The records of the stars he knows,
    and each
  Romance that round about the
    heavens lingers.
At dinner-time he oft delights to
    preach
  On which was made the first, or
    forks or fingers.

Indeed, all things he knows, or
    high or low—
  The things that fly on wing, or
    go a-walking—
Except one thing he never seems
    to know,
  And that's when he should stop
    his endless talking.

THE PERJURY OF A RE-JECTED LOVER

WHEN I was twenty-one, I swore,
    If I should ever wed,
The maiden that I should adore
    Should have a classic head;
Should have a form quite Juno-
        esque;
    A manner full of grace;
A wealth of hirsute picturesque
    Above a piquant face.

But I, alas! am perjured, for
    I've wed a dumpy lass
I much despised in days of yore,
    Of quite the plainest class,
Because each maiden of my dream,
    Whose favor I did seek,
Was so opposed unto my scheme
    I married Jane in pique.

MAID OF CULTURE

MAID of culture, ere we part,
Since we've talked of letters, art,
Science, faith, and hypnotism,
And 'most every other ism,
When you wrote, a while ago,
Ζώη μοῦ, σὰς ἀγαπῶ,

Let me tell you this, my dear :
Though your lettering was clear,
Though the ancient sages Greek
Would be glad to hear you speak,
They would be replete with woe
At your μοῦ, σὰς ἀγαπῶ.

For, dear maiden most astute,
You have placed the mark acute
O'er omega. Take your specs.
See? It should be circumflex.
Still I love you, even though
You have written ἀγαπῶ.

NOT PERFECT

HER eyes are blue—a lovely hue
  For eyes; her cheeks are pink,
And for the cheek, 'twixt me and
    you,
That color's right, I think.

Her fingers taper prettily,
  Her teeth are white as pearls—
Her hands seem softer far to me
  Than any other girl's.

Her figure's trim—it is petite—
  I like them just that way,
And truly, maiden half so sweet
  You'd not find every day.

And yet, alas! she's not my choice,
  This creature of my rhyme—
Because her soft and rich-toned
    voice
Is going all the time.

A CITY DWELLER'S WISH

I LOVE the leaf of the old oak-tree,
  I love the gum of the spruce,
I love the bark of the hickory,
  And I love the maple's juice.

On the walnut's grain I fondly dote,
  On the cherry's fruit I'd dine,
And I love to lie in a narrow boat,
  And scent the odor of pine.

Ah, me! how I wish some power
    grand
  Would invent some single tree
With all these points well devel-
    oped, and
  Would send that tree to me!

I'd plant it deep in the jardinière
  That stands in this flat of mine;
I'd give it the sweetest, tenderest
    care,
  And water its roots with wine.

WHERE ARE THEY?

WHAT has become of the cast-off
  coats
  That covered Will Shakespeare's
  back?
What has become of the old row-
  boats
  Of Kidd and his pirate pack?

Where are the scarfs that Lord By-
  ron wore?
  Where are poor Shelley's cuffs?
What has become of that wondrous
  store
  Of Queen Elizabeth's ruffs?

Where are the slippers of Ferdi-
  nand?
  Where are Marc Antony's clothes?

62

WHERE ARE THEY?

Where are the gloves from Antoi-
    nette's hand?
Where Oliver Goldsmith's hose?

I do not search for the ships of
    Tyre—
The grave of Whittington's cat
Would sooner set my spirit on fire—
Or even Beau Brummel's hat.

And when I reflect that there are
    spots
In the world that I can't find,
Where lie these same identical lots,
And many of this same kind,

I'm tempted to give a store of gold
    To him that will bring to me
A glass, Earth's mysteries to un-
    fold,
    And show me where these things
    be.

63

MEMORIES

Yon maiden once a jester did
    adore,
  Who early died and in the
    church-yard sleeps.
Once in a while she reads his best
    jokes o'er
  And sits her down and madly,
    sorely weeps.

A SAD STATE

I KNOW a man in Real Estate,
  Whose pride of self's sublime.
He'd like to be a poet great
  But " can't afford the time."

65

AD ASTRA PER OTIUM

As I read over old John Dryden's
verse,
 The rhymes of men like William
 Blake, and Gay,
The stuff that helped fill Edmund
Waller's purse,
 And that which placed on Mar-
 vell's brow the bay,

It doth appear to me that in those
times
 The Muses quaffed not sparkling
 wine, but grog,
And that to grow immortal through
one's rhymes
 Was 'bout as hard as falling off
 a log.

CONSOLATION

SHAKESPEARE was not accounted
   great
When good Queen Bess ruled Eng-
   land's state,
So why should I to-day repine
Because the laurel is not mine?

Perhaps in twenty-ninety-three
Folks will begin to talk of me,
And somewhere statues may be
   built
Of me, in bronze, perhaps in gilt,

And sages full of quips and quirks
Will wonder if I wrote my works.
So why should I repine to-day
Because my brow wears not the
   bay?

SATISFACTION

ON READING "NOT ONE DISSATIS-
FIED," BY WALT WHITMAN

GOD spare the day when I am satis-
    fied!
Enough is truly likened to a feast
    that leaves man satiate.
The sluggishness of fulness comes
    apace; the dulness of a mind
    that knows all things.
The lack of every sweet desire; no
    new sensation for the soul!
To want no more?
What vile estate is that?
What holds the morrow for the soul
    that's satisfied?
What holds the future for the mind
    content?
Is aspiration worthless?

Is much-abused ambition then so
    vile?
What is the essence of the joy of
    living?
Must yesterday, to-morrow, and to-
    day all be the same,
With nothing to be hoped for?
Is not a soul athirst a joyous thing?
Where lies content to him whose
    eye doth rest on higher things?
What satiation can compare to hope?
Yet who among the satisfied hath
    need of hope?
What can he hope for if he's satis-
    fied?
'Tis but conceit, and nothing more,
    to prate of satisfaction!
God spare the day when I am satis-
    fied!
I do not want the earth,
Yet nothing less will leave me quite
    content;
And once 'tis mine,
I'm very sure you'll find me roam-
    ing off
After the universe!

TO A WITHERED ROSE

THY span of life was all too short—
  A week or two at best—
From budding-time, through blos-
    soming,
  To withering and rest.

Yet compensation hast thou—aye!—
  For all thy little woes;
For was it not thy happy lot
  To live and die a rose?

THE WORST OF ENEMIES

I do not fear an enemy
Who all his days hath hated me.

I do not bother o'er a foe
Whose name and face I do not
   know.

I mind me not the small attack
Of him who bites behind my back:

But Heaven help me to the end
'Gainst that one who was once my
   friend.

JOKES OF THE NIGHT

BLESSED jokes of my dreams! Your
 praises I'd sing.
No mirth can compare to the mirth
 that you bring.
I've read London *Punch* from be-
 ginning to end,
On all comic papers much money
 I spend,
But naught that is in them can
 ever seem bright
Beside the rich jokes that I dream
 of at night.

How I laugh at those jests of my
 brain when at rest,
The gladdest and merriest, sweetest
 and best!

And how, when I wake in the morning and try
To call them to mind, oh how bash-
  ful, how shy
They seem, how they scatter and
  hide out of sight—
Those jokes of my dreamings, those
  jests of the night!

Take the one that came to me to-
  day just at dawn:
The Cable-Car turns and remarks
  to the Prawn,
"The Crowbar is seasick; but then
  what of that,
As long as the Camel won't wear
  a silk hat?"
I laughed—why, I laughed till my
  wife had a fright
For fear I'd go wild from that joke
  of the night.

And they're all much like that one
  —elusive enough,
Yet full of facetious, hilarious
  stuff—

JOKES OF THE NIGHT

Stuff past comprehension, stuff no
    man dares tell;
For nocturnal jests, e'en told ever
    so well—
'Tis odd it should be so—are not
    often bright,
Except to the dreamer who dreams
    them at night.

AN AUTUMNAL ROMANCE

A LEAF fell in love with the soft
    green lawn,
  He deemed her the sweetest and
    best,
And then on a dreary November
    dawn
  He withered and died on her
    breast.

75

THE COUNTRY IN JULY

WHERE glistening in the softness
   of the night
The vagrant will-o'-wisps do greet
   the sight;
Where fragrance baffling permeates
   the breeze
That gently flouts the grasses and
   the trees;
Where every flying thing doth seem
   to be
Instinct with sweetly sensuous mel-
   ody;
Where hills and dales assume their
   warmest phase,
With here and there a scarf of opal
   haze
To soften their luxuriant attire;
Where one can almost hear the el-
   fin choir

THE COUNTRY IN JULY

Across the meadow-land, down in
   the wood,
In songs of gladness—there are all
   things good.
Ah! ye who seek the spot where
   joys abide,
Awake! Awake! Seek out the
   country-side,
And through the blue-gray July
   haze see life
All free from care, from sorrow, and
   from strife.

MAY 30, 1893

It seemed to be but chance, yet
   who shall say
That 'twas not part of Nature's
   own sweet way,

That on the field where once the
   cannon's breath
Lay many a hero cold and stark
   in death,

Some little children, in the after-
   years,
Had come to play among the grassy
   spears,

And, all unheeding, when their romp
   was done,
Had left a wreath of wild flowers
   over one

MAY 30, 1893

Who fought to save his country,
  and whose lot
It was to die unknown and rest for-
  got?

79

THE CURSE OF WEALTH

"WHAT shall I put my dollars in?"
    he asked, in wild dismay.
  "I've fifty thousand of 'em, and
    I'd like to keep 'em too.
I'd like to put them by to serve
    some future rainy day,
  But in these times of queer fi-
    nance what can a fellow do?

"A railway bond is picturesque,
    and the supply is great,
  But strangely like a novel that
    upon occasion drags,
Of which the critics of the time in
    hackneyed phrases state,
  'The work has certain value, but
    the int'rest often flags!'

" The same is true of railway shares,
    'tis safer to invest
In ploughshares, so it seems to
    me, in this unhappy time.
Some think great wealth a blessing.
    but it cannot stand the test ;
He's happier by far than I who's
    but a single dime.

" He does not lie awake at night
    and fret and fume, to think
Of bank officials on a spree with
    what he's toiled to get.
He is not driven by his woe quite
    to the verge of drink
By wondering if his balance in
    the bank remains there yet.

" He does not pick the paper up
    in terror every night
To see if V.B.G. is up, or P.D.Q.
    is down ;
It does not fill his anxious soul
    with nerve-destroying fright
To hear the Wall Street rumors
    that are flying 'bout the town.

THE CURSE OF WEALTH

"Ah, better had I ta'en that cash
    that I have skimped to save,
And spent it on my living and
    my pleasures day by day!
I would not now be goaded nigh
    unto my waiting grave,
By wondering how the deuce to
    keep those dollars mine for aye.

"I'd not be bankrupt in my nerves
    and prematurely old,
These golden shackles must be
    burst; I must again be free.
What Ho without! My ducats—
    to the winds with all my gold,
That I may once again enjoy
    the rest of poverty."

THE RHYME OF THE AN-
CIENT POPULIST

IT was an ancient populist,
  His beard was long and gray,
And punctuated by his fist,
  He had his little say:
"This is the age of gold," he said,
"'Tis gold for butter, gold for bread,
Gold for bonds and gold for fun;
Gold for all things 'neath the sun."
        Then with a smile
        He shook his head.
        "Just wait awhile,"
        He slyly said.
"When we get in and run the State
We'll tackle gold, we'll legislate.
        We'll pass an act
        And make a fact
By which these gold-bugs will be
  whacked

Till they're as cold
As is their gold.
We're going to make a statute law
  by which 'twill be decreed
That standards are abolished, for a
  standard favors greed.
This is the country of the free, and
  free this land shall be
As soon as we the 'people' have
  our opportunity,
And he who has to pay a bill
Can pay in whate'er suits his will.
The tailor? Let him take his coats
    And pay his notes;
    Or if perchance
    He's long on pants,
    Let trousers be
    His £. *s. d.*
The baker! Let his landlord take
    His rent in cake,
Or anything the man can bake.
And if a plumber wants a crumb,
He may unto the baker come
        And plumb.
A joker needing hats or cloaks
Can go and pay for them with jokes,

THE ANCIENT POPULIST

And so on: what a fellow's got
Shall pay for things that he has not.
If beggers' rags were cash, you'd
  see
No longer any beggary;
In short, there'd be no poverty."
"A splendid scheme," quoth I; "but
  stay!
What of the nation's credit, pray?"
"Ha-ha! ho-ho!" he loudly roared.
"We'll leave that problem to the
  Lord.
And if He fails to keep us straight
Once more we'll have to legislate,
    And so create,
    Confounding greed,
As much of credit as we need."

ONE OF THE NAMELESS GREAT

I KNEW a man who died in days of
    yore,
  To whom no monument is like
    to rise;
And yet there never lived a mortal
    more
  Deserving of a shaft to pierce
    the skies.

His chiefest wish strong friend-
    ships was to make;
  He cared but little for this poor
    world's pelf;
He shared his joys with every one
    who'd take,
  And kept his sorrows strictly to
    himself.

F   86

IN FEBRUARY DAYS

FAIR Nature, like the mother of a
    wayward child
  Who needs must chide the off-
    spring of her heart,
Disguiseth for a season all the sweet
    and mild
  Maternal softness for an austere
    part.

And 'neath her frown the errant
    earth in winter seems
  Prostrate to lie, and petulant of
    mood;
Restrained in icy fetters all the
    babbling streams,
  Like naughty babes who're learn-
    ing to be good.

IN FEBRUARY DAYS

Then, in this second month, most
    motherlike again,
  The frown assumed gives now
    and then a place
To soft indulgent glances, lessening
    the pain,
  And hints of spring and pardon
    light her face.

A CHANGE OF AMBITION

Horatius at the bridge, and he
Who fought at old Thermopylæ;

Great Samson and his potent bone
By which the Philistines were
 slone;

Small David with his wondrous
 aim
That did for him of giant frame;

J. Cæsar in his Gallic scraps
That made him lord of other chaps;

Sweet William, called the Con-
 queror,
Who made the Briton sick of war;

A CHANGE OF AMBITION

King Hal the Fifth, who nobly
  fought
And thrashed the foe at Agincourt;

Old Bonaparte, and Washington,
And Frederick, and Wellington,

Decatur, Nelson, Fighting Joe,
And Farragut, and Grant, and, oh,

A thousand other heroes I
Have wished I were in days gone
  by—

Can take their laurels from my
  door,
For I don't want 'em any more.

The truth will out; it can't be hid;
The doughty deed that Dewey did,

In that far distant Spanish sea,
Is really good enough for me.

The grammar's bad, but, O my son,
I wish I'd did what Dewey done!

MESSAGE FROM MAHAT-MAS

ONSET BAY, MASSACHUSETTS, *May* 24, 18—. — The-osophists and others at Onset Bay Camp Grounds have been greatly excited of late by a message which has been received from the Mahatmas, Koot Hoomi, and his partner, who are summering in the desert of Gobi. The message is of considerable length, and contains much that is purely personal.—*Daily Newspaper*.

SOUND the timbrel, beat the drum!
Word from the Mahatma's come.
Straight from Hoomi Koot & Co.
Comes the note to us below,
Full of joy and gossiping.
Hoomi Koot is summering
In the desert waste of Gobi,
In a cottage of adobe.
All the little Koots are well.
Tommy Koot has learned to spell.
Mrs. Koot is busy on
Papers on "The Great Anon,"

Which by special cable soon,
From her workshop in the moon,
Will be sent to us below
By grand Hoomi Koot & Co.

We are told that Maggie Koot
Looks well in her golfing suit;
And her brand-new Astral Bike
Is the best they've seen this cike—
Cike is slang for cycle, so
I have learned from Koot & Co.
Soon she's going to take a run
Out from Gobi to the sun,
After which she thinks to race
For the Championship of Space,
And a trophy given by
The Grand High Pasupati.

Baby Koot has learned to walk,
And likewise, 'tis said, to talk;
But, to Mrs. Koot's dismay,
Seems to have a funny way:
Full of questions, "Why and How,"
All about the sacred cow.
Questions of a flippant ilk,
Like "Is Buddha made of milk?"

Questions void of answers spite
Of his parents' second sight.
What to do with Baby Koot
Worries all the whole cahoot.

Finally the message ends
With best love to all our friends.
Give our enemies a twist.
Let each true theoso-fist
Strike a thunder-hitting blow
For the firm of Koot & Co.;
Strike till black is every eye
Doubting our theosophy.
And impress on every tribe
Now's the season to subscribe.
Guard against the coming storm;
Keep our astral bodies warm.
Give us bonnets for the head;
Keep our spirit stomachs fed.
Let your glad remittance go
Out to Hoomi Koot & Co.,
Through their Agents on the earth,
Men and women full of worth;
And when next a message comes
From the Koots down to their
    chums,

MESSAGE FROM MAHATMAS

Those who've paid their money
  down
Will receive a harp and crown.

Step up lively! now's the time
For your nickel and your dime,
To provide for winter suits
For the grand Mahatma Koots.
Furthermore, be not too brash,
Send it up in solid cash.
Astral money, it may be,
Circulates in theory;
But 'tis best to give us cold,
Bilious, drossy, filthy gold.

All our blessings to you go.
Yours, for health,
           H. Koots & Co.

THE GOLD-SEEKERS

Gold, gold, gold!
What care we for hunger and cold?
What care we for the moil and strife,
Or the thousands of foes to health
    and life,
When there's gold for the mighty,
    and gold for the meek,
And gold for whoever shall dare
    to seek?
    Untold
    Is the gold;
And it lies in the reach of the man
    that's bold:
In the hands of the man who dares
    to face
The death in the blast, that blows
    apace;
That withers the leaves on the
    forest tree;
That fetters with ice all the north-
    ern sea;

95

That chills all the green on the
fair earth's breast,
And as certainly kills as the un-
stayed pest.
It lies in the hands of the man
who'd sell
His hold on his life for an ice-
bound hell.
What care we for the fevered
brain
That's filled with ravings and
thoughts insane,
So long as we hold
In our hands the gold?—
The glistening, glittering, ghastly
gold
That comes at the end of the
hunger and cold;
That comes at the end of the
awful thirst;
That comes through the pain and
torture accurst
Of limbs that are racked and minds
o'erthrown,
The gold lies there and is all our
own,

Be we mighty or meek,
If we do but seek.
For the hunger is sweet and the
cold is fair
To the man whose riches are past
compare;
And the o'erthrown mind is as
good as sane,
And a joy to the limbs is the rack-
ing pain,
If the gold is there.
And they say, if you fail, in your
dying day
All the tears, all the troubles, are
wiped away
By the fever-thought of your shat-
tered mind
That a cruel world has at last
grown kind;
That your hands o'errun with the
clinking gold,
With nuggets of weight and of
worth untold,
And your vacant eyes
Gloat o'er the riches of Paradise!

ODE TO A POLITICIAN

ALL hail to thee, O son of Æolus!
All hail to thee, most high Borean
   lord!
The lineal descendant of the Winds
   art thou.
Child of the Cyclone,
Cousin to the Hurricane,
Tornado's twin,
      All hail!
The zephyrs of the balmy south
      Do greet thee;
The eastern winds, great Boston's
   pride,
In manner osculate caress thy mas-
   sive cheek;
      Freeze onto thee,
And at thy word throw off con-
   gealment
And take on a soft caloric mood;
And from afar,
From Afric's strand,

ODE TO A POLITICIAN

Siroccan greetings come to thee!
The monsoon and simoom,
In the soft empurpled Orient,
At mention of thy name
Doff all the hats of Heathen-
  dom!
And all combined in one vast ag-
  gregation,
Cry out hail, hail, thrice hail to
  thee,
Who after years, and centuries, and
  cycles e'en,
Hast made the winds incarnate!
        To thee
        The visible expression in
          the flesh,
        Material and tangible,
Of all that goes to make the ele-
  ment
That rages, blusters, blasts, and
  blows!
And if the poet's mind speaks
  true,
If he can penetrate their purposes
  at all,
It is not far from their intent

ODE TO A POLITICIAN

To lift thee on their broad Novem-
    ber wings
        So high
That none but gods can ever hope
Again to gaze upon thy face!

SOME ARE AMATEURS

SHAKESPEARE was partly wrong—
  the world's a stage,
  This is admitted by the bard's
  detractors.
Had William seen some Hamlets
  of this age
  He'd not have called *all* men
  upon it actors.

LITTLE BOOKS
BY FAMOUS WRITERS

THE FIRST CHRISTMAS (From " Ben-Hur ")   *By Lew. Wallace*

THE STORY OF THE OTHER WISE MAN
By Henry van Dyke

TWO GENTLEMEN OF KENTUCKY
By James Lane Allen

EPISODES IN VAN BIBBER'S LIFE
By Richard Harding Davis

GOOD FOR THE SOUL
By Margaret Deland

EVELINA'S GARDEN
By Mary E. Wilkins

COBWEBS FROM A LIBRARY CORNER
(Verses)   *By John Kendrick Bangs*

THE WOMAN'S EXCHANGE
By Ruth McEnery Stuart

THE CAPTURED DREAM
By Octave Thanet

STORIES OF PEACE AND WAR
By Frederic Remington

Uniform with this Volume—with Frontispiece
Fifty Cents a Volume

HARPER & BROTHERS, PUBLISHERS
NEW YORK AND LONDON
☞ *Any of the above works will be sent by mail, postage prepaid, to any part of the United States, Canada, or Mexico, on receipt of the price.*

Reprint Publishing

For People Who Go For Originals.

This book is a facsimile reprint of the original edition. The term refers to the facsimile with an original in size and design exactly matching simulation as photographic or scanned reproduction.

Facsimile editions offer us the chance to join in the library of historical, cultural and scientific history of mankind, and to rediscover.

The books of the facsimile edition may have marks, notations and other marginalia and pages with errors contained in the original volume. These traces of the past refers to the historical journey that has covered the book.

ISBN 978-3-95940-054-1

www.reprintpublishing.com

www.ingramcontent.com/pod-product-compliance
Lightning Source LLC
Chambersburg PA
CBHW070827250626
47170CB00006B/2231